Published by Clever Fox Press Group:

Ordering Informaiion:

Quantity sales. Special discounts are available on quantity purchases by schools and charitable organizations. For details, please contact the same super talented person mentioned above.

The Story of Rugby Town in 15 Tail Wags
Fox, Julie G.
Kvirikashvili, Lika
Bulbeck, Leonora
Nel, Rene

WELCOME TO RUGBY CV21

HEART OF ENGLAND

To our left, we see Rugby School.
It is one of the oldest schools in
the country and in the world. Many years ago,
Dr Thomas Arnold, its most famous headmaster,
turned Rugby School into the model for other
schools by making very important educational
reforms, which quickly spread all around the world.
He introduced history, mathematics, modern
languages and games into the curriculum.
He also put an end to bullying. How did he do it?
Dr Arnold gave sixth formers, the oldest pupils
in the school, the power to run the school
alongside the teachers and administrators.
A very smart move!

On the right, we see the old building of Rugby Radio Station. It was the biggest radio station in the world when it was built, and it became the home of the first international telephone call, which took place between the town of Rugby and the town of Houlton in the state of Maine in the United States of America. The radio station also transmitted messages to military submarines all over the world, and it was used to send telegraph messages between countries. The old building stood empty for a long time after the radio station was closed, but very, very soon, a new school will open inside this amazing historic building. How cool is that?

The school is for the children of a new town, called Houlton, which is being built now on the outskirts of our town. Houlton will be an important part of Rugby very soon. But one hundred years ago, my other ancestor, Tommy the Learned Cat the Third, was sitting right in front of the big, clever machine called the telegraph and was sending important messages all the way to Australia, the United States of America, India, New Zealand and lots of other countries. Those were the times before smartphones and computers were invented, so the telegraph was the only way to communicate with the world.

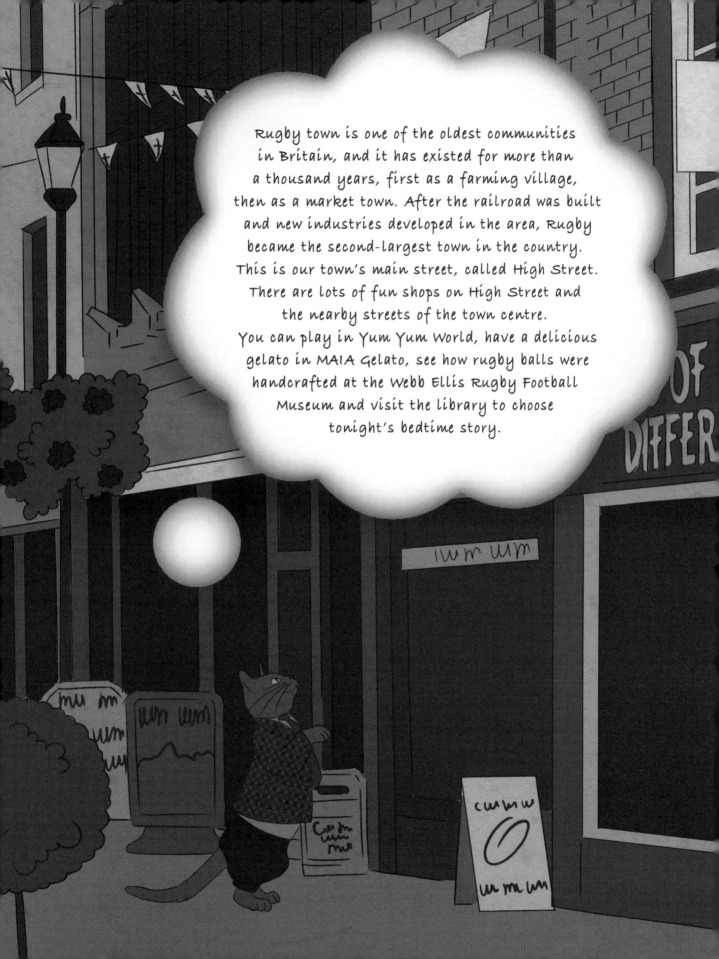

Rugby town is one of the oldest communities in Britain, and it has existed for more than a thousand years, first as a farming village, then as a market town. After the railroad was built and new industries developed in the area, Rugby became the second-largest town in the country. This is our town's main street, called High Street. There are lots of fun shops on High Street and the nearby streets of the town centre. You can play in Yum Yum World, have a delicious gelato in MAIA Gelato, see how rugby balls were handcrafted at the Webb Ellis Rugby Football Museum and visit the library to choose tonight's bedtime story.

Check out this huge rugby ball.
A few of them appeared on
the streets of our town to celebrate
the World Cup which England hosted in
the autumn of 2015. Pupils from local schools
created the artwork for the balls. The Rugby
World Cup is the most important tournament
in the sport of rugby union, and it happens
every four years. The competition is one
of the biggest sporting events in
the world, just like the World Cup
and the Olympics.

And now let's look to the left.
This is Caldecott Park, one of my favourite
places in Rugby town. The playground is the place
I always run to first, but sunbathing and napping
on the tennis courts or bowling green are not
a bad way to pass the time either. In the summer,
I love the craft fairs (all those handmade cat toys
are amazing!) and art exhibitions (I am a big fan
of the arts, having learned to paint with all four
of my paws and a tail). Musical performances
on the bandstand are my absolute favourite.
I find a spot on a nearby tree and meow in tune.
If you want to hang out in Caldecott Park,
come down any afternoon of the week,
rain or shine.

Tonight, right after our tour,
why don't you join me at Rugby Theatre,
on the left. There is a new play on, and
you guys are all invited. But I have to make
one stop before that, at Salters of Rugby.
This famous shop has been a part of Rugby town
centre for over one hundred and thirty years.
That's where Rugby School pupils used to order their
uniforms. But way before that, both Rugby School
pupils and teachers, as well as all the other
residents of our town, came to Salters to buy
their fancy suits and hats, as well as
other important accessories every
gentleman had to have.

RUGBY

tage & Screen

THE WEDDING VIE

The C.A.T.S. KIDZ

IMAGINARIUM

Look to your left, and you will see
a statue of Thomas Hughes right next
to Rugby School's beautiful library building.
Thomas Hughes was a well-known author,
as well as a lawyer, a judge and a politician.
He is most famous for his novel
Tom Brown's School Days, which is based
on his own experience of studying at Rugby School
while the great Dr Thomas Arnold
was the headmaster there.
Tom Brown's School Days was the first
school novel ever written.
It is a great book.

Famous author J. K. Rowling said that *Tom Brown's School Days* inspired her to write *Harry Potter*. Rugby School is not Hogwarts, of course, but some pupils have told me that magic does happen there very often, especially in the Macready Theatre where pupils put on fabulous plays and musicals.

The Soldier
Rupert Brooke, 1887 - 1915

If I should die, think only this of me:
   That there's some corner of a foreign field
That is for ever England. There shall be
   In that rich earth a richer dust concealed;
A dust whom England bore, shaped, made aware,
   Gave, once, her flowers to love, her ways to roam,
A body of England's, breathing English air,
   Washed by the rivers, blest by suns of home.

And think, this heart, all evil shed away,
   A pulse in the eternal mind, no less
     Gives somewhere back the thoughts by England given;
Her sights and sounds; dreams happy as her day;
   And laughter, learnt of friends; and gentleness,
   In hearts at peace, under an English heaven.

RUPERT BROOKE
1887 - 1915

Small shops and independent
businesses are so important in our community.
Look to your left, and you will see Mister Robinson's
Barbershop on Church Street. This is not just
the best barbershop in our town, and Mr Robinson
is not only one of the best barbers out there,
but he is also the most amazing person.
He helps homeless people by giving free haircuts
to boys and girls, and free beard trims to their dads,
uncles and grandpas who bring food and clothes
for a homeless charity. Would you like to have
a free haircut? Bring some food and clothes to
help a homeless person, especially during cold
seasons when homeless people in our
community need all the help
they can get.

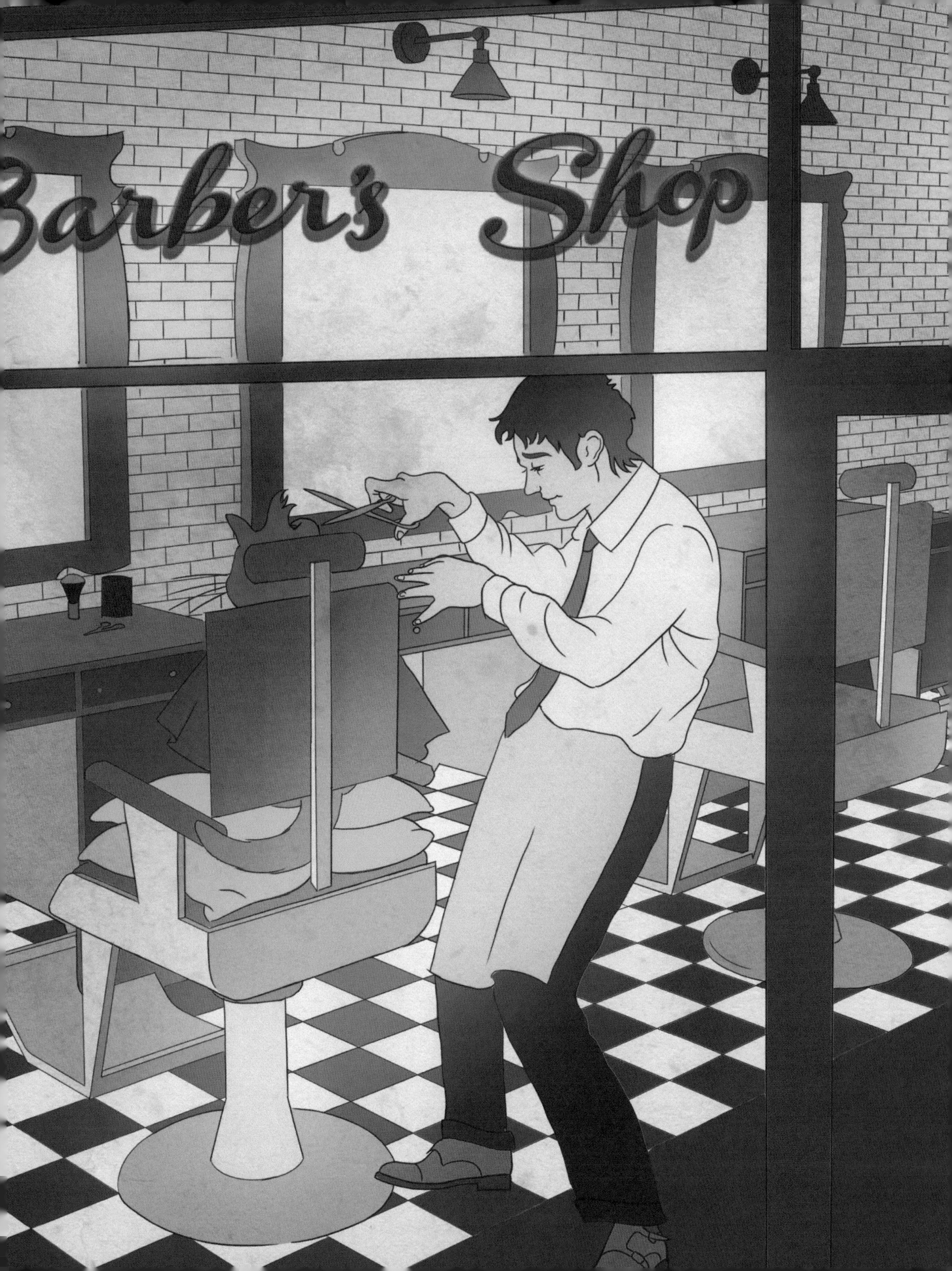
arber's Shop

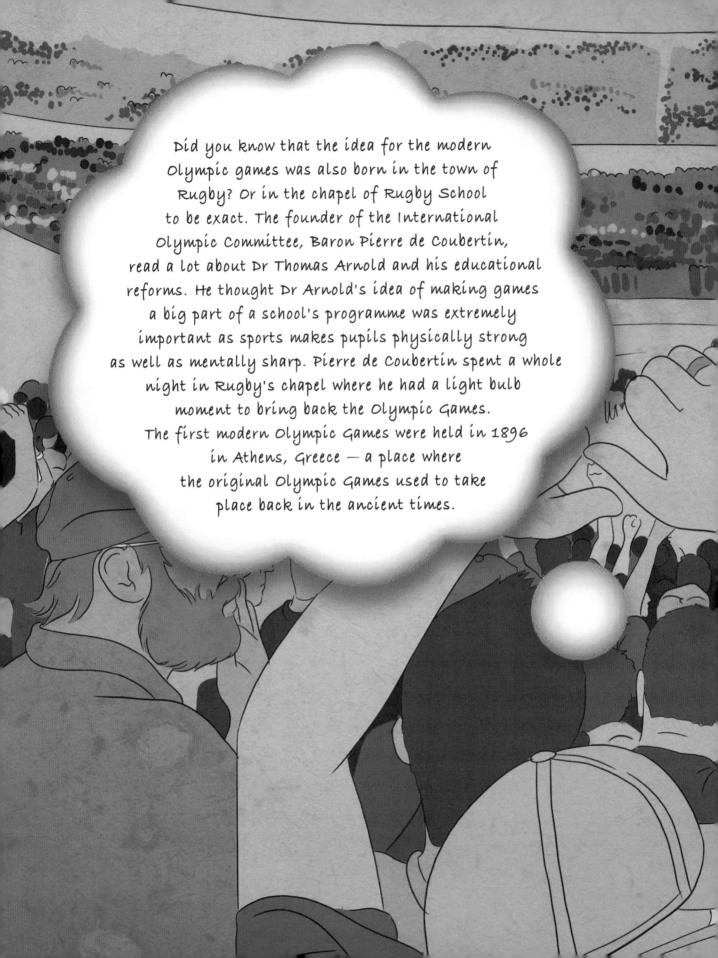

WILLIAM WERR ELLIS

1266 - 1872

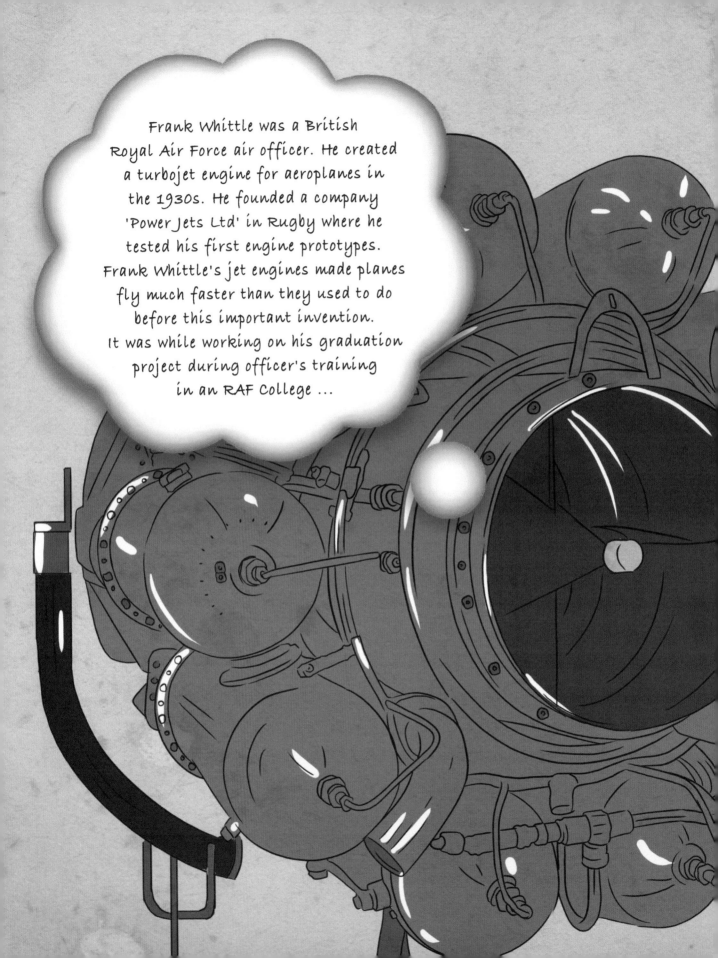

Printed in Great Britain
by Amazon